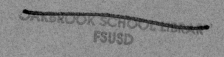

Los Angeles Clippers

Richard Rambeck

CREATIVE EDUCATION

Published by Creative Education
123 South Broad Street, Mankato, Minnesota 56001
Creative Education is an imprint of The Creative Company

Designed by Rita Marshall

Photos by: Allsport Photography, Associated Press/Wide World Photos,
NBA Photos, and UPI/Corbis Bettmann.

Photo page 1: Loy Vaught
Photo title page: Lorenzen Wright

Library of Congress Cataloging-in-Publication Data

Rambeck, Richard.
Los Angeles Clippers / Richard Rambeck.
p. cm. — (NBA today)
Summary: Describes the background and history of the Los Angeles
Clippers pro basketball team.
ISBN 0-88682-877-5

1. Los Angeles Clippers (Basketball team)—Juvenile literature.
[1. Los Angeles Clippers (Basketball team)—History. 2. Basketball—
History.] I. Title. II. Series: NBA today (Mankato, Minn.)

GV885.52.L65R36 1997   96-6532
796.323'64'0979494—dc21

Once a small Spanish mission town located between the San Gabriel Mountains and the Pacific Ocean, Los Angeles has grown into the second-largest city in the United States. More than 3 million people live within the city limits of Los Angeles. In addition, almost 15 million reside within 50 miles of the middle of the city.

Los Angeles is a center of commerce and wealth in the United States. Its location makes it one of the key gateways to the Asian ports of Japan, China, and Korea. But the business L.A. is best known for is show business. The city is the

Bob McAdoo starred when the franchise was in Buffalo.

Future Hall of Famer Dolph Schayes was the first coach of the Buffalo Braves.

movie and television capital of the world. Many young actors and actresses have moved to the area, hoping to become stars. Other people have been drawn to the region by the sunny weather and the miles and miles of beaches. For the past century, Los Angeles has been a place to seek fame, fortune, and fun.

It is not surprising, then, that Los Angeles has also attracted several professional sports teams away from other cities. Both of L.A.'s professional basketball teams, for example, began playing elsewhere. The Los Angeles Lakers started in Minneapolis and decided to change addresses in 1960. Although the Lakers were successful in Minneapolis, they became an even bigger hit once they moved to Los Angeles. Everyone in L.A., it seemed, became a Laker fan.

Despite the Lakers' tremendous popularity in Los Angeles, the owners of the San Diego Clippers decided in 1984 that L.A. basketball fans could support two teams in the National Basketball Association (NBA). So the Clippers moved north for the 1984–85 season. "We're hoping to follow in the Lakers' footsteps," said Clippers president Alan Rothenberg. "We feel that Los Angeles is big enough to handle two NBA success stories."

But the Clippers have yet to write a Laker-type success story in their new home. The team has been haunted by injuries and bad luck. Some of the players that the club counted on to lead it forward have had to retire for medical reasons, or have left the Clippers via trades or free agency for other NBA squads.

In the 1990s, the Clippers have a roster packed with such young stars as Lorenzen Wright and Brent Barry, and such

Hard-driving forward Ken Norman.

key veterans as Pooh Richardson and Loy Vaught. The club has also brought in Bill Fitch, a coach with a history of winning, to provide solid direction for the players. Clippers fans are hoping this talented cast can bring the team the type of success its crosstown rivals have had.

1 9 7 1

Bob Kauffman led the Buffalo Braves in scoring, assists, and rebounding.

THE BUFFALO SHUFFLE

The best days of the Clippers franchise were actually spent far from the West Coast—in Buffalo, New York. During the mid-1970s in Buffalo, in fact, the club recorded three of the four winning seasons in its history and its only playoff appearances. The team's nickname was the Braves then, and the stars of the squad were high-scoring center Bob McAdoo, speed demon guard Randy Smith, and flashy ball handler Ernie DiGregorio.

But even Buffalo Braves fans had to suffer through a few losing years at first. The Braves were added to the NBA as an expansion team for the 1970–71 season. They staggered to a 22–60 record behind the limited talents of such players as Bob Kauffman, Donnie May, and Emmette Bryant. After the season ended, team management was determined to build a contender by adding top young players through the college draft.

In the first few rounds of the 1971 draft, Braves leaders selected players they were sure could help their team right away, such as 7-foot center Elmore Smith and guard Fred Hilton. In the seventh round, team officials decided to take a gamble. They chose Randy Smith, a local college star and great all-around athlete from Buffalo State University. The gamble paid off.

"We really didn't expect Randy to make our team," explained Braves general manager Eddie Donovan. "When you're drafting that far down, you're looking to give a local kid a chance who might not get one." Smith was a raw, unproven talent. Even though he was only 6-foot-3, Smith played forward in college because of his jumping ability and because he lacked ballhandling skills. In the pros, Smith struggled at first, but the Braves found a place for his considerable talents.

Team coach Jack McCarthy used Smith mostly as a defensive specialist at first, but the young player worked hard and soon developed solid shooting and passing skills. When Jack Ramsay took over as coach in 1972, he gave Smith a little more playing time. "There is not a man in the league who can run with him," Ramsay explained. "He's amazing. As far as pure physical ability, I haven't seen anyone in the league to match him."

With his speed and jumping ability, Smith made life difficult for some of the better guards in the league. "I hate guarding him," said New York Knicks All-Star guard Walt Frazier. "Even when he isn't scoring, he's running so fast all over the place, and I have to chase him."

Smith also had confidence to match his athletic talents. "People have always come to me and said, 'Randy, I didn't think you could do it,'" Smith recalled. "I always say, 'Well, I thought I could.'"

1 9 7 2

Elmore Smith was named to the NBA All-Rookie team, the Braves' first postseason honor.

Randy Smith, a franchise star in the 1970s.

Danny Manning, a scoring leader in the early 1990s.   11

Randy Smith began an NBA-record streak of 10 seasons without missing a single game.

Randy Smith may have been sure of his own ability, but Buffalo fans weren't as sure of their club's ability to succeed. Ramsay's first Buffalo team posted a dismal 21–61 record. The one bright spot during the 1972–73 season was the play of rookie center Bob McAdoo, a 6-foot-10, 225 pounder from the University of North Carolina. McAdoo averaged 18 points a game for the Braves and was named NBA Rookie of the Year. But that was just the beginning. "Big Mac" would win the league scoring title the next three seasons, averaging more than 30 points a game each time. Along with Smith, point guard Ernie DiGregorio, and forward Jim McMillian, McAdoo turned Buffalo into a playoff team.

Clearly the key to the Braves' offense, McAdoo believed that the only bad shot was one he didn't take. McAdoo could hit jumpers from all over the court, or he could use his quickness to score inside. "I used to think he took bad shots, but I've changed my mind," explained Los Angeles Lakers center Kareem Abdul-Jabbar. "Nobody takes shots from where McAdoo does and hits like he does."

Boston Celtics forward John Havlicek called McAdoo "the best pure shooter I've ever seen." Phoenix Suns forward Curtis Perry said Big Mac's jump shot was "just about like radar."

To McAdoo, scoring came as naturally as breathing. "It is hard not to get buckets in this league," he chuckled. "If I was doing any less, people would think I'm dogging it."

McAdoo had two great offensive weapons, the first of which was a deadly accurate shooting touch. "I don't worry about being long or short with my shot," McAdoo explained.

"I just want to be on line." Big Mac's second weapon was an amazing quickness for a man of his size. He used his speed to get away from those who tried to guard him. "A man will watch him [McAdoo] getting open," said Buffalo assistant coach Tates Locke. "He'll watch him be open. And he'll still be watching him after Mac's open and scored the basket. That's how quick he is."

Led by McAdoo, the Braves became one of the most exciting and entertaining teams in the league. But the big center and his teammates wanted more—they wanted to be champions. It was a realistic goal, because the Braves still hadn't reached their peak. Unfortunately, Buffalo could never get past the early rounds of the playoffs, particularly when the club had to take on the best team of the time, the powerful Boston Celtics. The Braves and Celtics waged tremendous battles during the 1974 and 1976 playoffs, but each time Boston emerged victorious, and Buffalo went home without a championship trophy.

Despite these disappointments at the hands of the Celtics, things never looked brighter for the Braves franchise than after the 1975–76 season. Then dark clouds moved in very quickly. First, Jack Ramsay left Buffalo to become head coach of the Portland Trail Blazers. He was replaced by Tates Locke, who was soon replaced by Bob MacKinnon. MacKinnon was then replaced by Joe Mullaney. The revolving door applied not just to coaches, but also to players. Jim McMillian and Ernie DiGregorio were both traded. Even Bob McAdoo was sent packing to the New York Knicks, a move that shocked and saddened Buffalo fans.

The once-promising Braves, with all their young stars, had

Adrian Dantley was named NBA Rookie of the Year his final year with the Clippers.

become one of the worst teams in the league. The only bright spot during the horrible 1976–77 campaign was the play of Adrian Dantley, a rookie drafted out of Notre Dame. The 6-foot-5 forward averaged 20.3 points a game and was named NBA Rookie of the Year. Amazingly, Dantley was traded at the end of the season to the Indiana Pacers, who then traded him to the Los Angeles Lakers. Every one of the former Braves stars, except Randy Smith, was now gone. And also, apparently, were the fans. Buffalo's attendance fell to an average of only 6,000 people per game during the 1977–78 season. In the off-season, the owners of the team decided the franchise would be better off moving from snowy Buffalo to sunny San Diego.

THE BRAVES SAIL TO CALIFORNIA

The Buffalo Braves moved west and became the San Diego Clippers. "It's a clean slate, a fresh start, and we're excited about it," said new coach Gene Shue. But how excited were the citizens of San Diego going to be? The Southern California city had been home to an NBA franchise during the late 1960s. That team moved to Houston because it wasn't getting enough support. San Diego had also been home to two franchises in the old American Basketball Association (ABA) during the early 1970s. Both teams had folded.

It seemed likely that the San Diego Clippers would also fail. The club that came from Buffalo was a ragtag collection of castoffs and unproven players. San Diego's training camp featured 41 free agents and rookies. "All these new faces, it's like raising another family," said Shue. The "family" included

The amazing Bob McAdoo.

former All-Star forward Sidney Wicks, powerful forward Kermit Washington, and guard Lloyd Free, an outstanding offensive talent.

Free was a colorful character who could talk as well as he could shoot. "People come right out of their seats when I do my thing," Free boasted. "People want to see that razzle-dazzle. They like seeing guys taking crazy shots and hitting them." Free's nickname was "World," as in "All-World." In fact, he later legally changed his name to World B. Free. During the 1978–79 season, Lloyd Free lived up to his nickname. He and Wicks led the Clippers to a 43–39 record in their first year in San Diego. The team missed the playoffs by one victory, but the Clippers had won 16 more games than they did the previous year, when they were still the Buffalo Braves.

1 9 7 9

World B. Free's average of nearly 29 points per game ranked second best in the NBA.

Rebounding leader Swen Nater.

The team had gone from the no-hope Braves to the high-hope Clippers in one season. Those hopes rose even higher after San Diego announced a major trade on May 13, 1979. The Clippers sent several players and draft choices to the Portland Trail Blazers in exchange for 6-foot-11 center Bill Walton. Walton was a huge talent. He had led Portland to the 1976–77 NBA title and was named the league's Most Valuable Player the following year. But he was also injury-prone, having missed much of the previous two seasons because of foot and knee injuries.

Powerful shooter Freeman Williams led the Clippers with 19.3 points per game.

"If Bill remains healthy," Gene Shue said excitedly, "I have every reason to think that the Clippers can be right in the thick of the title run." But Walton couldn't stay healthy. In his first three years as a Clipper, he played in only 14 games. The Clippers had gambled and given away a lot of talent to get Walton, and the gamble didn't pay off. The Clippers fell once again to the bottom of the league standings. To try to shake things up, the management fired Gene Shue and replaced him with Paul Silas. The team's luck still didn't change, however. San Diego even lost 19 straight games during the 1981–82 season.

The Clippers won only 25 games the following year, but the season had its bright spots. Bill Walton returned and showed flashes of his old form. In addition, first-year forward Terry Cummings out of DePaul University won the Rookie of the Year award by averaging almost 24 points per game. Cummings led the club in scoring again in the 1983–84 season, with a 22.9 points-per-game average. He was ably backed by point guard Norm Nixon, who averaged 17 points and 11.1 assists a game.

Bill Walton, a legendary star (pages 18–19).

Rookie Terry Cummings quickly became San Diego's top scorer, defender, and rebounder.

But the San Diego fans never really took to the Clippers. In their six seasons in San Diego, the Clippers made bad trades, had bad luck, and were just plain bad most of the time. One example of the team's poor judgment was when the Clippers traded young forward Tom Chambers to Seattle for center James Donaldson and forward Greg Kelser. Chambers became an All-Star in Seattle. Donaldson struggled with the Clippers and eventually was traded to Dallas, where he became a long-time starter.

The hard-luck Clippers moved to Los Angeles at the start of the 1984–85 campaign, but their fortunes didn't change much. First, young star Terry Cummings was sent to Milwaukee in exchange for Marques Johnson, who had been a college star in Los Angeles at UCLA. Cummings became an All-Star for Milwaukee. Johnson, meanwhile, had problems

Shot-blocking star Tom Chambers.

with his back and neck that continually kept him out of the lineup and eventually ended his career. Then point guard Norm Nixon, the team's floor general, suffered an Achilles tendon injury and eventually was forced to retire. This was another example of the Clippers' bad luck with trades. They had sent young guard Byron Scott to the Los Angeles Lakers to get Nixon, who had only one healthy season with the Clippers. Scott, on the other hand, wound up helping the Lakers win three NBA titles.

1 9 8 5

For the second straight year, All-Star Norm Nixon led the Clippers in assists.

CAGE HELPS THE CLIPPERS REBOUND

Not all of the Clippers' personnel decisions were bad ones. In the 1984 draft, they found a gem in forward Michael Cage, who had played college ball at San Diego State. Cage wasn't a great natural athlete, but he was a hard worker who never quit. He grew up in West Memphis, Arkansas, and was one of the few boys in his neighborhood to play basketball.

Cage and his best friend, Keith Lee, spent most of their time on the basketball court. "Keith and I didn't go to those [basketball] summer camps," Cage recalled. "We worked on each other. Sometimes he'd play me like it was a fight. I liked that." Cage and Lee were teammates in high school, playing on a team where, according to Cage, "no rebound was safe." Both players had plenty of offers from colleges to play basketball. Lee accepted a scholarship to go to Memphis State. Everyone assumed that his best friend would also go to the nearby college. But Cage had other ideas.

Even though his parents wanted him to stay close to

Mr. Rebound: Michael Cage.

home, Cage was impressed with San Diego State coach Smokey Gaines and decided to play his college ball on the West Coast, a long way from Arkansas. At San Diego State, Cage became one of the top scorers in the country. It was his rebounding, though, that most impressed the pro scouts. Cage loved to crash the boards—it was his pride and joy. "Moses Malone told me that if you went after them all, one night you might get every rebound," Cage recalled.

Cage was one of the few bright spots for the Clippers during their first few seasons in Los Angeles. The 1986–87 team won only 12 games and lost 70, the second-worst record in the history of the NBA. The following year the Clippers won only 17 games, but Cage led the league in rebounding. Despite his heroics, Cage was not in the Clippers' plans for the future. He was traded after the 1987–88 season to the Seattle SuperSonics for rookie point guard Gary Grant.

Grant wasn't the only player the Clippers picked up for the 1988–89 season. Los Angeles used the first choice in the 1988 draft to select Danny Manning, a player some experts called the best all-around talent to come out of college in years. He had led the underdog Kansas Jayhawks to the 1988 NCAA title.

When the 1988–89 season started, both Manning and Grant were in the starting lineup. Grant ran the offense, and Manning teamed with fellow forward Ken Norman and center Benoit Benjamin to give the Clippers a solid front line. Backing up Manning and Norman on the forward corps was another rookie, Charles Smith from Pittsburgh.

Less than halfway through the 1988–89 campaign, Manning damaged his knee while attempting a layup. The injury

1 9 8 6

Derek Smith was the Clippers' top scorer for the second season in a row.

23

to Manning was disastrous both for the young star and for the Clippers' offensive strategy. It did have one bright side, however. With Manning out of the lineup, Charles Smith got an opportunity to demonstrate to fans in L.A. and around the league what he could do. The 6-foot-10 power forward showed a lot of promise, averaging almost 17 points a game.

Charles Smith was one of only 16 players in the league to score 1,500 points and grab 500 rebounds.

RON HARPER MAKES A STRONG COMEBACK

Charles Smith played even better during the 1989–90 season, averaging 21.1 points and 6.7 rebounds a game. Only one other player, guard Ron Harper, had a higher scoring average for the Clippers that year. Harper had been acquired from Cleveland earlier in the year in exchange for the rights to forward Danny Ferry, who was taken with the second pick in the 1989 draft. Ferry chose to play in Italy rather than sign with Los Angeles. Harper had an immediate impact on the Clippers, averaging 23 points, 5.7 rebounds, and nearly five assists per game. Then the Clippers' bad luck surfaced again. Midway through the year, and fewer than 30 games into his career in L.A., Harper suffered almost the same injury that had knocked Danny Manning out of the lineup a year earlier. Some fans were convinced that this team had a hex on it.

When the 1990–91 season started, however, the team was optimistic. Danny Manning was healthy again. Forwards Charles Smith and Ken Norman were consistent performers. The on-again, off-again talents of center Benoit Benjamin appeared to be in the on position. Benjamin was the key to the Clippers' success, the experts said. The Los Angeles players knew that Benjamin was important, but they believed the key guy was a player still recovering from a major injury: Ron Harper.

"Until he came, we were all so undecided about who would take the last shot, who would do this or do that," explained Gary Grant. Most of the Clippers were used to losing. Harper wasn't. "He was the missing piece," Benjamin said. "He brought a winning attitude. I mean, we all had an attitude, but he'd been a winner." Harper, though, wasn't quite ready to play when the 1990–91 season started. His knee was still injured.

Gary Grant's average of 8.6 assists per game ranked him eighth in the league.

A former All-Star player in Cleveland, Harper worked hard to rehabilitate his knee. "This injury isn't something you want to hurry up," Harper said. "I don't want to just come back and be another NBA player. I want to come back at the level that I left." That level was what the Clippers were counting on to lead them to the playoffs.

Unfortunately for the Clippers and for their fans who came to the Los Angeles Sports Arena to watch them play, the 1990–91 season was another disappointment. Harper did come back and showed that the injury hadn't robbed him of his abilities. Smith and Norman also had solid years. But the team decided that its other frontline player, Benoit Benjamin, would be better off playing somewhere else. The moody center's contract was up at the end of the season, and it was unlikely that he would choose to stay with the Clippers. Los Angeles traded the 7-foot-1 Benjamin to Seattle for center Olden Polynice and two first-round draft choices.

Polynice brought a hustle and desire that Benjamin had

Top rebounder Loy Vaught (pages 26–27).

rarely shown as a Clipper. Los Angeles didn't make the play-offs in 1990–91, but the team had definitely improved.

1 9 9 2

Coach Larry Brown steered the Clippers to a 23–12 finish and their first playoff berth since 1976.

LOOKING TOWARD THE FUTURE

During the rest of the 1990s, Los Angeles acquired what they hoped would turn out to be some of the best young players in the league—this team had high hopes for the future. To direct their squad of young players, Clippers management brought in Larry Brown—a proven winner in both the college and professional ranks. Clippers fans hoped that coach Brown would provide the veteran leadership needed to help turn this collection of young players into a smooth-running team. Brown, with nearly 25 years of college and professional coaching experience in both the ABA and NBA, came to the Clippers with only one losing season on his record. But he had a reputation for not staying long in any one place. A writer for the *Los Angeles Times* once said that Brown would make the Hall of Fame, but "with a suitcase under his bust."

Overshadowing Brown's nomadic disposition was his reunion with Danny Manning—Brown's star player when their team won an NCAA championship at Kansas. Brown's arrival coincided with Manning's ascension, as Manning led the Clippers in scoring for three years in a row, etching out a reputation as one of the top NBA players.

Brown did nothing to tarnish his reputation as a winner. In his first year as coach, he led the Clippers to their first playoff berth since 1976. The Clippers lost in five games to the Utah Jazz in the first round, but returned to the playoffs in Brown's second year. They lost again in the first round, this time to the powerful Houston Rockets. During this time, rumors abounded that Manning and Brown weren't getting along, and Brown—true to his reputation for not sticking around—resigned at the end of the year.

Midway through the following season, Manning was traded to the Atlanta Hawks for aging star Dominque Wilkins, and the Clippers again looked like they were falling into their bad habit—poor trades and losing seasons. Though they hired Bill Fitch—a coach who had a reputation as a strong rebuilder—and acquired a fat handful of top draft picks, the Clippers were unable to gel. As they struggled through the 1996–97 season with no team leader, it became clear that their best hopes for the future rested on the shoulders of Brent Barry and on the raw talent of rookie Lorenzen Wright.

Guard Pooh Richardson led the club in assists (5.4) for the second consecutive season.

Barry, son of Hall of Famer Rick Barry, attracted attention around the league when he won the Slam-Dunk Championship during the 1995–96 All-Star Weekend. Reminiscent of such NBA superstars as Julius Erving and Michael Jordan, Barry took off from the free throw line for the winning shot.

"I think he's going to be a really good player," said veteran teammate Pooh Richardson. "He's getting used to the pro game and it's going to take some work. But I think he's the kind of guy who will work."

"I feel I have to work on my complete and entire game," said Barry. "That's basically what my father and both of my brothers have stressed. To continue to work hard, to continue to progress as a player, to not stop learning about the game."

Brent Barry, an improving young talent.

Lorenzen Wright, the Clippers' center of the future.

*Rodney Rogers
grabbed five steals
in a game against
Portland, matching
his career high.*

If the Clippers are going to succeed, Fitch knows that Barry will need help from Wright, who came to the Clippers as a sophomore out of Memphis. "Lorenzen is typical of a guy who comes out early," said Fitch. "He's a little bit behind. He's had a lot thrown at him—I don't know how much of it's sticking. But he is one heck of a kid. He wants to do well."

If Clippers' management can be patient enough to allow Fitch to bring around the team the way he has with other teams in the past, and if veterans Loy Vaught and Pooh Richardson can teach the nuances of the NBA to Barry and Wright, then maybe the Clippers' potential on paper can be turned into victories on the court. The team appears to be headed in the right direction. Although downed by Utah in the first round of the playoffs, the Clippers made their opponents work hard for the wins, an indication that there are better things to come for the "other" L.A. team.